Copyright © 1987 Nord-Süd Verlag, Mönchaltorf, Switzerland
First published in Switzerland under the title Der Traumbaum
English text copyright © 1987 Anthea Bell
Copyright English language edition under the imprint
North-South Books © 1987 Rada Matija AG, Faellanden, Switzerland

First published in the United States, Great Britain, Canada,
Australia and New Zealand in 1987 by North-South Books, an
imprint of Rada Matija AG.

Distributed in the United States by
Henry Holt and Company, Inc., 521 Fifth Avenue,
New York, New York 10175.
Library of Congress Cataloging in Publication Data

Wolf, Winfried, 1943–
The dream tree.

Translation of: Der Traumbaum.
Summary: Michael banishes the ghosts, witches,
giants, and magicians that surround his bed keeping
him from sleep, sending them to a desert island with
a beautiful dream tree.
[1. Sleep--Fiction. 2. Bedtime--Fiction.
3. Monsters--Fiction] I. Schlüter, Manfred,
1953– ill. II. Title.
PZ7.W8193Dr   1987   [E]   87-1593

ISBN 0-8050-0488-2

Distributed in Great Britain by
Blackie and Son Ltd, 7 Leicester Place,
London WC2H 7BP.
British Library Cataloguing in Publication Data

Wolf, Winfried
The dream tree.
I. Title II. Schlüter, Manfred III. Der
Traumbaum. *English*
833'.914[J]   PZ7

ISBN 0-200-72915-2

Distributed in Canada by
Editions Etudes Vivantes, Saint-Laurent.

Distributed in Australia and New Zealand by
Buttercup Books Pty. Ltd., Melbourne.
ISBN 0 949447 51 X

Printed in Germany

By Winfried Wolf

THE DREAM TREE

Translated by Anthea Bell

Illustrated by Manfred Schlüter

For Griffin, who loves stories about dreams.
xxo
Mommy

North-South Books

Michael was lying in bed.
But he just couldn't sleep.
He kept seeing ghosts and witches
and giants and magicians.
They prowled round his bed, howling,
chuckling, muttering and whispering.

"Go away!" Michael shouted.
But the ghosts and witches
and giants and magicians
just laughed.

"Please, please leave me alone!"
Michael begged them. "I'm tired,
and I want to go to sleep."

But they only made horrible faces
and laughed louder than ever.
At that, Michael lost his temper.
"If you don't go away at once,"
he shouted, "I'll cast a magic
spell and send you off to a tiny
island in the middle of the sea."

The ghosts and witches and giants
and magicians roared with laughter.

"Very well," said Michael,
"if that's how you want it. I'm
going to shut my eyes and
think you all away."

Then a strong wind rose, seizing
the ghosts and witches and giants
and magicians.
It whirled them up and up, high up
into the clouds. Then they went
plunging down again, down and down,
until they all landed on the
sandy shore of the tiny island.
    The ghosts and witches wailed.
The giants and magicians moaned.
    On the island grew a single tree.
It reached right up to the clouds,
and you could hardly see the top of it.
But its flowers were so beautiful
that they shone down on the island.
They were blue and yellow,
crimson and gold and lilac.

When the ghosts and witches and giants and magicians had recovered from their shock, they saw the flowers.

"We want them! We must have them!" hissed the magicians, waving their magic wands.

But none of their spells would work. The flowers were still out of reach.

"Tee hee hee!" chuckled the witches spitefully. "Tee hee hee! Those magicians can't work any magic at all. We'll sit astride our broomsticks and ride up to the top of the tree."

And up they flew.

But as their greedy hands reached out for the wonderful flowers, their broomsticks suddenly bent, and the witches tumbled off and fell to the ground.

Their broomsticks were broken. The flowers were still out of reach.

"Whoooooo!" howled the ghosts.
"We'll scare that tree so badly
it will fall down in a fright!
And then the flowers will be ours,
all ours!"
   They held each other by their
fluttering sleeves and danced
around the tree, howling horribly
until they were hoarse.
But the tree stood exactly where it was.

"Ho, ho! What weaklings you all are!"
said the boastful giants. "We'll just
pull the tree down."
And they spat on their hands,
and took hold of the tree.
The giants' hands were soon sore.
But the tree stood exactly where it was.

Then the witches screeched,
"We witches are clever!
We have a plan.
Let's all stand on top of each other.
Giants at the bottom, and the rest
of us will climb up on them,
and then we'll have those flowers!"
    So the biggest giant stood at the
foot of the tree. The next
biggest climbed on his shoulders,
and then the next biggest and so on.
The last giant almost reached
the top of the tree.
Then one of the magicians climbed
up all the giants, reached his hand
out for the flowers – and whoosh!
All of a sudden, the tree grew
a little taller. And the flowers
were still out of reach.

Then the other magicians climbed up,
and so did the ghosts,
and last of all the witches.
But whenever any of them tried
to pick one of the wonderful flowers,
the tree grew a little taller, and
their hands grasped empty air.

   All of a sudden, the giant at the
bottom felt his strength give way.
He tottered, and they all fell
down on the sand. And the
flowers were still out of reach.

"How silly you all are!" laughed
Michael, tucked up in bed.
"You'll never reach the flowers,
because that tree is mine.
I'm the one who imagined it.
And if your heads weren't full of
nasty thoughts, you could do the same.
It's very easy; you just shut your
eyes and think of something nice.
But now you'll have to stay on
the desert island for ever."
The ghosts, witches, giants and
magicians wailed miserably.

But Michael closed his eyes
and went to sleep.